*To Simone, Rebecca, Alessandro,
and everyone with a good heart.*

The Heart of Winter
Somos8 Series

© Text and illustrations: Alessandro Montagnana, 2024
© Edition: NubeOcho, 2024
© Translation: Cecilia Ross, 2024
www.nubeocho.com · hello@nubeocho.com

Revised by: Caroline Dookie & Rebecca Packard

Original title: *Cuore d'Inverno*

First edition: September, 2025
ISBN: 978-84-19253-56-9
Legal Deposit: M-6492-2024

Printed in Spain.

All rights reserved. Reproduction is strictly prohibited.

The Heart of Winter

Alessandro Montagnana

Chip and his siblings loved to perch on telephone wires during the winter months.

From up there they could watch the snowflakes drifting down, and they could swing back and forth in the breeze.

On Christmas Eve, a heavy storm rolled in. All the little robins took to the sky, flying off in search of shelter.

But a sudden gust of wind blew Chip backwards, and he lost the others.

"Wait for me!" he cried. The wind drowned out his voice.

Chip flapped with all his might to catch up,

but it was too much for him...

And, exhausted, he fell.

Chip could see no sign of his siblings. He couldn't even guess which way they might have gone.

Then he spied a house in the distance. Could they have taken shelter there?

At that very same moment, Lula was inside the house looking out her window, and she saw him.

Without thinking twice, she hurried outside and invited Chip in. She offered him her friendship.

Lula lived alone, and she was very happy to have company.

Chip and Lula spent the afternoon decorating the house and the tree with Christmas ornaments.

Later, while playing outside, Chip discovered that Lula's nose was the perfect spot for watching snowflakes.

The two of them had
a lot of fun together.
They built a snow fox
and a snow bird.

They had snowball fights
and played outside for hours.
It was an unforgettable
afternoon.

But right before sundown,
the young robin sighed wistfully.

Lula asked what was wrong.
Chip was, in fact, feeling homesick.

Just then, they realized someone was watching them.

They looked up and saw that they were surrounded by robins.

"You found me!" Chip exclaimed, flying joyfully up to his brothers and sisters.

She missed Chip.
She would have loved
to celebrate Christmas
with him.

Lula was thinking about
the previous Christmases
when she heard a sudden
knock at the door…

It was Chip! He'd come back to share something very important with her:

his and his family's friendship.

And in their hearts they knew,
without a doubt, that this would be

the best Christmas ever.